We All Like Different Things
and that's
A-OK
with Me!

By Jo Dodd and Joseph Dodd
Illustrated by Jenifer Novak Landers

For Dad, Mom,
Deon, Drew
and Ethan - you
all like
different
things, and
that's A-OK
with me! Love,
Joseph

Follow @livinginjotopia on Instagram to hear more about
Jo and Joseph's books
Copyright 2021 by Jo Dodd
Illustrations by Jenifer Novak Landers
All rights reserved. Permission to reproduce any selection
from this book must be granted in writing from the author.
Jotopia Productions, LLC.
The text of this book is set in Kristen ITC
The art is digital illustrations.
Library of Congress Catalogue-in-Publication Data is on file.
ISBN: 978-1-7366082-4-1

Hi, my name is Joseph
and I'm nine years old!

I look just like my Dad
or at least,
that's what I'm told!

Here are my brothers
and this is Dad and Mum
They say I'm spoiled
Since I'm the youngest son!

My family is big and we all

like different things.

Drew likes basketball

and Ethan likes to sing!

Deon likes music

and I love to cook!

Dad's a football coach
and Mum writes books!

We're all so different
and yet we get along.

It's like we're all singing
a slightly different song.

You see, I like ketchup
But it makes Dad sick.
I don't like hot sauce
But for Dad it does the trick!

It's like, Ethan can't stand cheese

and eggs make Deon gag!

If Mum gave Drew a banana
he'd hide it in her bag!

Mum can't stand beans
but why I just can't see,

We all like
different things
and that's
A-OK with me!

It's like, I like soccer
and riding on my bike!

Mum likes reading books

and going on a hike.

Dad loves watching sports

and laughing really loud!

Ethan dyes his hair red!
You wouldn't miss him in a crowd!

Drew likes
baking cookies

and Deon loves
climbing trees!

We all like different things
and that's A-OK with me!

So if you think
you don't fit in
and there's no one else
like YOU

Think about this poem
and remember
that it's true,

...that everyone is different,
It's OK we're not the same.

Life would be so boring
if we all played just one game!

Think about
this poem
and say it
loud and free

We All Like Different Things

and that's
A-OK
with Me!

Join us on social media
We would love to hear from you!

@livinginjotopia

Learn about other books by Jo: www.livinginjotopia.com

Out now: *Tilly Toad's Heavy Load*
Coming soon: *Take That, Fear! You Can't Keep Up With Me!*

Author Notes:
In my opinion, some of the best books are those that stem from real-life situations or conversations, as often we can resonate with the story being told. This book came from a wonderful conversation with my youngest son Joseph, in June of 2020 during a time when there was a lot of darkness in the world around us and things seemed very bleak.

We had just watched the movie "Trolls World Tour" which, if you've not seen it, is a movie all about embracing differences and seeing things from a different perspective. Joseph and I were driving in the car, listening to the soundtrack. The music must have made him think about the movie as, out of nowhere he suddenly said,

"Mom - think about it, we all like different stuff, right? And that's OK!"

When I asked him what he was talking about, he went on to say:

"Well, you see Mom, it's like this. I like ketchup, but Dad hates ketchup. He likes BBQ sauce, and I don't like BBQ sauce, because, well you see Mom, I like ketchup! And Ethan, well, Ethan doesn't like cheese, and you LOVE cheese, Mom, right? And then there's Drew. Drew doesn't like bananas. I mean, Mom, how do you NOT like bananas? But Drew doesn't like them, and so that's OK with me. And then there's Deon. Deon hates eggs! How can he hate eggs, Mom? Eggs are delicious! But that's OK, because Deon likes ketchup, so it's OK. But do you see Mom, do you see what I'm saying?!"

What he didn't see was me fighting back tears. Somehow he knew I needed that 'lightness'. I needed a laugh and a child's perspective that made everything in that moment feel better. I was so touched by the conversation that I posted about it on social media. My lovely friend Jane (who with her family owns the best bookshop in the world, Gullivers Bookshop in Wimborne, Dorset UK) read the post and commented "he summed it up perfectly. It sounds to me like he just wrote a children's book!"

. . . and the rest as they say, is history!